Grandad's Concrete Garden

Shoo Rayner

Young Lions

Best Friends · Jessy and the Bridesmaid's Dress ·
Jessy Runs Away · **Rachel Anderson**
Changing Charlie · Clogpots in Space · **Scoular Anderson**
Ernest the Heroic Lion-tamer · **Damon Burnard**
Weedy Me · **Sally Christie**
Something Old · **Ruth Craft**
Almost Goodbye Guzzler · Two Hoots · **Helen Cresswell**
Magic Mash · Nina's Machines · **Peter Firmin**
Shadows on the Barn · **Sarah Garland**
Clever Trevor · Nora Bone · **Brough Girling**
Private Eye of New York · Sharon and Darren · **Nigel Gray**
The Thing-in-a-Box · **Diana Hendry**
Desperate for a Dog · Houdini Dog · **Rose Impey**
Georgie and the Dragon · Georgie and the Planet Raider ·
Julia Jarman
Cowardy Cowardy Cutlass · Free With Every Pack ·
Mo and the Mummy Case · The Fizziness Business ·
Robin Kingsland
And Pigs Might Fly! · Albertine, Goose Queen · Jigger's Day Off ·
Martians at Mudpuddle Farm · Mossop's Last Chance ·
Michael Morpurgo
Grubble Trouble · **Hilda Offen**
Hiccup Harry · Harry Moves House · Harry's Party · Harry with Spots On ·
Chris Powling
Grandad's Concrete Garden · **Shoo Rayner**
The Father Christmas Trap · **Margaret Stonborough**
Pesters of the West · **Lisa Taylor**
Jacko · Messages · Rhyming Russell · **Pat Thomson**
Monty, The Dog Who Wears Glasses · Monty Bites Back ·
Monty must be Magic · Monty – Up To His Neck in Trouble ·
Colin West
Ging Gang Goolie - It's An Alien! ·
Stone the Crows, It's a Vacuum-cleaner · **Bob Wilson**

First published in Great Britain by
A & C Black (Publishers) Ltd 1994
First published in Young Lions 1994

Young Lions is an imprint of HarperCollins Children's Books,
part of HarperCollins Publishers Ltd,
77/85 Fulham Palace Road, London W6 8JB

Text and illustrations copyright © 1994 Shoo Rayner
All rights reserved.

ISBN 978-0-00-674-849-6

Chapter One

There are two really good things about living in Little-Blinkey-on-Sea.

1. The beach.

2. My grandad lives just round the corner.

My grandad is always busy doing
something interesting and he'll ask
if I want to help.

It wasn't always like that.
He used to go to work every day.

Thursday...Friday... then the weekend off... Wednesday... Tuesday... before coming... for over forty years... back again on Monday, again and again...

At lunchtime he'd eat his sandwiches.

All morning he would add up numbers.

Then he'd add up some more numbers until it was time to go home.

Then he

RETIRED!

On his last day at work he had a leaving party.

His boss gave him a clock for his mantelpiece and a card with a deep and meaningful message on it, which got Grandad thinking.

Hmm... that's made me think.

Smile
Tomorrow is the first day of the rest of your life...

Good Luck!

To celebrate his retirement, Grandad took Gran on a cruise round the Greek islands.

They sent postcards from all the islands they visited.

STATUS OF OLD GREEK

OBNOXOS

DOMESTOS

ATHOS

LIPGLOSS

PORTHOS

M.S. DOS

GREEK RUINS

RACEHOSS

N
W E
S

All the cards said the same thing.

When they got back home, Grandad found his retirement card on the mantelpiece. It made him think.

'Now I've got no work to go to,' he muttered to himself, 'I must find something to occupy my time'.

Gran overheard him and stuck her head round the door.

You can start by sorting out the garden.

Hmm.

But that was not what Grandad had in mind at all.

Chapter Two

Over the next few weeks, Grandad had a go at all sorts of hobbies.

He tried

... but it made him feel dizzy.

He was good at water-skiing
. . . until he remembered he
couldn't swim.

He tried
rock-climbing,
but he kept
falling off.

Pot-holing
made him feel
claustrophobic.

He decided to look for a quieter
hobby.

He was no good at photography.

He tried lace-making and knitting, but he just got into a tangle

He tried to write his memoirs,

but he couldn't think of anything to say beyond page two.

'I must find something to occupy myself,' he sighed.

The garden needs a good sorting out.

But that was not what Grandad had in mind.

You see the garden was more of a yard. Not many plants grow well by the sea, so there were just a few tough old weeds poking through the gravel.

You couldn't even get a fork into the ground.

Then, one Saturday morning,
Grandad phoned me up.

Come on over, lad.

'I know what to do with the
garden,' he said.

But you hate
gardening,
Grandad.

Ha ha, yes! But
I saw this really
interesting programme
on TV. What we
need is a
feature.

So off we went on a trip round the garden centres.

The first one only had gnomes and tubs.

The second garden centre had lots
of lovely things:

gazebos   benches

arches

dovecots.

I think
not!

SPLAT!

The third garden centre was a bit
ecological.

They had
wind-pumps,

compost-bins,

and worm-bins.

Everything was solar powered or
recycled. All their plants were
good for curing illnesses.

HERB SIXPENCE
Good for coughs, colds,
warts, verrucas, piles,
runny tummy and
bad memory.

Then we found The Fountain Centre.

MEGAFOUNTAIN
If you have to ask the price,
You probably can't afford it!

Needless to say, the mega-fountain was far too expensive and wouldn't fit into the car boot. But Grandad did buy a fountain.

It had a spouting dolphin

a shell

a little boy to hold it up

a pump

and a base.

It was all made of plastic but it looked like real stone. Grandad was very pleased with it.

Chapter Three

I suppose that was the beginning of
Grandad's obsession! The next day
a truck arrived with

a new spade

a new fork

a pile of sand

three bags of cement

and a little garden hut to put it
all in.

Grandad dug a trench and laid a special electric cable from the house to a hole in the garden.

I helped Grandad mix up the concrete and we poured it into the hole.

Soon the hole was filled up and smooth on top. The electric cable was poking out of the middle.

After a few days the concrete was hard enough for the fountain to be installed.

We all stood looking at it.
Gran thought it was very nice
but it was a *bit* small. Grandad
looked troubled.

There was quite a lot of sand and cement left over, which gave Grandad an idea.

What's needed is a plinth.

(That's a sort of base that lifts up the thing you want to show.)

We made the plinth out of chicken-wire . . .

and then we sort of threw wet concrete at it. We had a great time.

We went to the beach and collected thousands of seashells.

Grandad set to work, modelling the wet cement. Then he let me press in the seashells.

We put the fountain on top.
Gran liked it
(once Grandad
had put some
clothes on the
water-
nymphs).

Grandad,
it's brilliant!

Grandad was pleased but he already had his eye on the shed.

Hmm.... maybe I could turn it into a Greek temple.

He ordered more sand, cement and chicken-wire and hired a mixer, too. It worked away all day long.

GLOBBITY GLOB

Grandad wrapped the shed in chicken-wire and we threw wet concrete all over it.

Before long he had it looking very grand and classical.

That's what I call a shed!

Now Grandad had got the hang of it, there was no stopping him.

The mixer was churning away for weeks. Grandad started on the big stuff:

archways

statues

palm trees.

He made birds, animals and
flowers.

He would write mottoes into the
wet cement, like

and other uplifting messages.

Then he painted all the things he'd made so that they looked incredibly realistic.

It was hard to walk past Grandad's garden and not notice all the changes. People started to lean over the wall and make comments.

Miss Gothorpe, who ran the local art society said 'It's quaint but it's not Real Art. Concrete is far too common for Real Art.'

Yeeurgh...nasty concrete.

Grandad's next-door neighbour.

It's a frightful eyesore...lowers the tone of the area... I'm surprised they let him build it.

Grandad's neighbour hasn't got much of a sense of humour!

The garden became quite famous.
People must have told their friends
about it because more and more of
them came to look. Cars would slow
down as they came past.

Coach-loads of sightseers stopped to stare at the garden.

A man came and took some photographs and turned them into a postcard.

Chapter Four

Grandad was beginning to think about charging people to come in and see the garden when, one morning, a man arrived from the council. He had a good look round.

He hummed and hahed.

Then he said,

The council man delved into his briefcase and brought out a pile of papers. Then he took a deep breath.

When the man had left, Grandad
told us what he had said.

Gran told Mrs Herbert who lives
down the street . . .

Mrs Herbert told Mr Smith at the
newsagent . . .

Mr Smith told a friend of his, who
works for the newspaper . . .

And before you could shout,
'I protest,' there was a long
persistent ring on the doorbell.

Well, Grandad made his statement
to the press.

Of course that's not quite what
Smudge wrote!

LITTLE WEEKLY

VOL 93 – No. 32

Local man will fight to the death.

by Danny Smidgen.

Battling Grandad, Art Granby, pictured at home yesterday.

Battling grandad, Art Granby, (65), last night told me of his fight with Little Blinkey Council to keep his 'concrete garden.' "I will fight to

BLINKEY ARGOS

Some of Mr. Granby's amazing statues.

Little Blinkey Council spokesman said: 'No Comment.' The concrete gar-

next-door neighbour said: 'I think it's a real eyesore. It's not

When Grandad read the paper he could hardly believe it.

But it was too late. This was just the kind of story the press could get their teeth into. The next time the doorbell rang, there was a crowd of reporters on the doorstep.

45

Grandad should have learned not to talk to newspaper reporters. But he thought he should try to explain things.

It was that tricky word 'Art' that really stirred up trouble. 'Art' was Grandad's nickname.

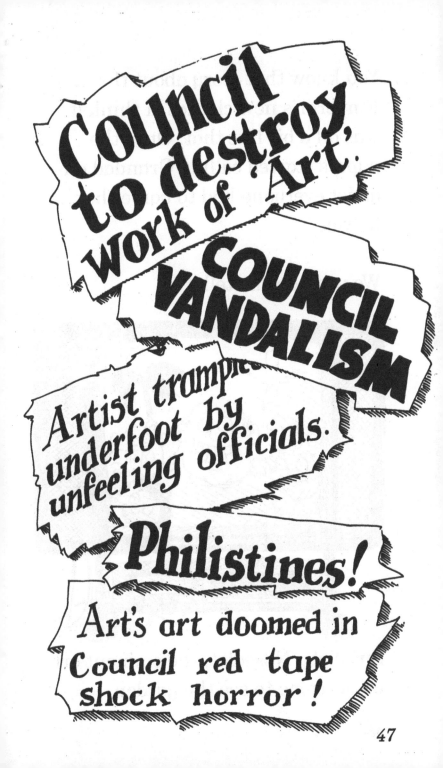

Council to destroy, Work of 'Art'.

COUNCIL VANDALISM

Artist trampled underfoot by unfeeling officials.

Philistines!

Art's art doomed in Council red tape shock horror!

You know that story about the Emperor's new clothes? I think it was all a bit like that. Once the papers started calling Grandad an artist everyone had to agree that he was.

We were on the telly!

Sir Digby Nosealot, the eminent art critic, came to see the garden.

There were lights and cameras and
Sir Digby waved his hands about
and said 'Marvellous!' a lot.

Now that the garden was
'nationally important,'
Miss Gothorpe came round again.
She waved her hands around
and said, 'Marvellous,' too!

Superb technique!

Marvellous modelling!

Ingenious colour scheme!

She was determined that
Grandad's garden
should be saved
and she started
up a campaign.

Save Grandad's Garden

Everyone signed the petition.

Petition
to Save Grandad's Concrete Garden.

Signature	Address
J. Smith	27. Rosehip Gardens
M. Mouse.	No. 3, Disneyland- U.S.A. !
(signature)	Doctor's Surgery. *(scribble)*
B Blinkinsop.	flat 2. Acacia Avenue
N. Bonaparte.	the Pines, Fir Tree Rd, Elba.
A.C. Black.	35 Bedford Row. London
Y. Lions.	Fulham Palace Rd., London.
R. McDonald.	The Burger's, High St., MK 42.

Some people didn't sign their real names!

There was a poster campaign.
Some of the posters were funny.

ARTISTS
DO IT IN
CONCRETE

Some were ordinary.

SAVE
GRANDAD'S
Concrete Garden

Art for 'Art's' sake!

Some were really boring.

LITTLE BLINKEY YOUNG ACCOUNTANTS' CLUB
SAY NO! to Council oppression.
SAY YES! to GRANDAD'S
CONCRETE GARDEN

Everyone joined in to save
Grandad's garden. There was even
a huge protest march to the
Town Hall

But the council weren't going to give in. They posted a notice on Grandad's front gate.

It said:

We had a week before they came to knock down all Grandad's work.

Grandad wasn't going to give in
either. He rebuilt the wall right
round the house and put a
portcullis in the gate. Where it used
to say 'Mon Repose,' it now said

He made fierce
looking
gargoyles
to frighten the
council men
and he put lights everywhere in
case they came at night.

When the demolition team arrived,
Grandad was ready for them.

Grandad stood his ground.
At eleven o'clock he drank some tea
through a straw.

The nation held its breath as
midday approached and the TV
stations went live.

Tick tock.

The police got restless.

Tick tock.

The council man
got nervous.

Tick tock.

Grandad was as
cool as a cucumber

In the distance,
we could hear the
town hall clock
strike twelve.

A gasp went up from the crowd as
the digger started moving.

The digger inched forward but, as the sound of the clock's bell died away, a new sound could be heard. It was the sound of sirens, and they were getting louder.

wee wah, wee wah, wee wah, blee blah, nee nah, wooooooooo

The digger reached the wall.

The crowd parted and a big black car, with a flag on it, eased through. There were two police motorbikes with it.

A man got out
and shouted.

HALT!

It was the Minister for Art. Once
the digger had been switched off he
made a speech for the TV cameras.
He said, 'Marvellous,' a lot too!

After full consultation,
and long consideration,
I have decided to save
this marvellous work
of art....... this great
monument of our times,
for the nation and for
the future.

So now Grandad is a famous artist. His work can be seen all over the place.

Outside the White House.

Outside the shopping centre.

Outside factories.

He was even asked to build a
tropical island outside the
Ministry of Art.

But his concrete garden is still the
best thing he ever did. So if you're
driving on the motorway and you
see a sign that says

LITTLE BLINKEY
(For Castle Granby)
NEXT LEFT
1 Km

Why not come and
visit us?

There's a new sign
by the gate
that says

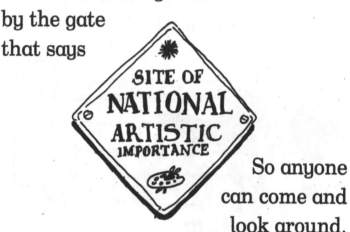

So anyone
can come and
look around.

Grandad's usually off in his studio
or in some exotic place making a
statue. But I'll probably be here
and I'd be pleased to show you
round.

www.ingramcontent.com/pod-product-compliance
Ingram Content Group UK Ltd.
Pitfield, Milton Keynes, MK11 3LW, UK
UKHW020215190625
459827UK00005BB/667